Fox Makes Friends

Adam Relf

Macmillan Children's Books

Fox sat in his room.
He was bored.
"I know," he said.
"I need a friend."

Fox picked up his net and went to see his mum.
"I'm going to catch a friend," he declared.
"You can't catch friends," Mum explained.
"You have to *make* friends."
So Fox put down his net and
set off to make a friend.

"What can I make a friend out of?"
he thought.

He picked up some sticks, an apple
and some nuts, and fixed them all
together. At last he had a brand new
friend standing in front of him.

"Are you my friend?" Fox asked,
but the friend said nothing.
  "Will you come and play?" he said,
but the friend didn't move."Maybe he's
too small," Fox thought. "I need to make
a bigger friend!"

Just then a rabbit ran by.
"Excuse me," said Fox. "I'm trying
to make a friend but this one is
too small. Can you help me
make a bigger one?"
"OK," said Rabbit.

They worked together and picked up a turnip,
some tomatoes, and some twigs. They stuck them
all together and had an even bigger friend
standing before them.

"Will you be our friend?" they asked,
but there was no answer.

"Will you come and play?" they said,
but the friend just stood there.
"Maybe he's still too small,"
said Rabbit.

A moment later Fox and Rabbit heard giggling in the treetops. It was a squirrel.

"What a mess you two are making!" he laughed.

"Well, if you can do better, come down and help us!" said Fox

"OK," said Squirrel.

This time all three of them set to work.
They picked up two huge pumpkins,
some branches and some apples.
They put them all together and made
the biggest friend that they could make.
 "Are you our friend?" they asked.
"Please will you come and play?"
But there was no reply.

Finally they all gave up.
"Oh well," said Fox. "I suppose I will never be able to make a friend."

Just then Fox's mother
came by.

"Hello," she said. "Who are
all your new friends?"

"Oh," said Fox. "My plan
didn't work. We made friends
but they won't play with us."

"Not them!" giggled his mother.
"These friends!" she said,
pointing to Squirrel
and Rabbit.

Fox looked over at Squirrel and Rabbit, and suddenly realised that he had been making friends all along!

So Fox, Squirrel, and Rabbit played for the rest of the day, and they stayed friends forever.

First published 2005 by Macmillan Children's Books
This edition published 2006 by Macmillan Children's Books
a division of Macmillan Publishers Ltd
20 New Wharf Road, London N1 9RR
Basingstoke and Oxford
Associated companies worldwide
www.panmacmillan.com

Produced by Fernleigh Books
1A London Road, Enfield
Middlesex EN2 6BN

Text copyright © Fernleigh Books 2005
Illustrations copyright © Adam Relf 2005

ISBN-13: 978-1405-05563-5
ISBN-10: 1-405-05563-4

1 3 5 7 9 8 6 4 2

A CIP catalogue record for this book is available from the British Library.

Manufactured in China